T0417809

THE OCEAN IS EVERYONE'S BUT IT IS NOT YOURS

McSWEENEY'S
SAN FRANCISCO

This is the sixth in a series of stories that will, god willing, someday become something larger, called *The Forgetters*.

Cover illustration by Annie Dills.

ISBN: 978-1-963270-02-0

These numbers could mean anything, or nothing:
10 9 8 7 6 5 4 3 2 1

www.mcsweeneys.net

Printed in Canada

THE OCEAN IS EVERYONE'S BUT IT IS NOT YOURS

by

DAVE EGGERS

McSWEENEY'S

For Amanda Uhle

AURORA GOT TO the waterfront early, hoping to glean some intel from the fishermen. This time of year, humpbacks were guaranteed and orcas were around, but you wouldn't necessarily see either every day. Dolphins were in abundance, and seals, and sea lions. But what would make any season was a blue whale. They saw only a few every year off Monterey, and afterward Aurora couldn't sleep. The blues were far grander, stranger than any photo could convey. They were planetary in their size and volume, their slow and ponderous ways. They were impractical, defenseless, absurd, and as smooth as river stones. They were underwater zeppelins that did not belong to this world. Aurora hadn't seen one in a year.

Her father, Marv, arrived at eight. His fly was open. "Dad," she said, and nodded toward it.

He smiled, turned from her, and resolved the issue.

"Ant says there were about twenty humpbacks seen off Santa Cruz yesterday," he said.

"Yup," Aurora said, pretending she knew this, too, but the fact was that her father still had sources of information she couldn't tap. It was another reason he was useful, even in his retirement.

He'd been the captain of the *Seeker* for thirty-four years before handing her the keys two years ago. In retirement he'd gotten bored, though, and had begun drinking each day at noon, and had been found asleep in his car, outside a movie theater, one February afternoon. He had not been driving, he would not do that, but when two cops tapped on his car window, he'd stepped out too quickly, drunkenly, tripped over his seat belt and broke his collarbone. In the ambulance he'd had a heart episode that put him in the hospital for two weeks.

Aurora wanted to get him out of the house and keep him sober, so she brought him back to the *Seeker* in a kind of emeritus role, where she could keep an eye on him. She had expected the experiment to be disastrous, but it had worked out beautifully. He never second-guessed her, and puttered around the ship like an elder statesman, eating licorice and drinking Fanta. He'd regressed to some childhood version of himself, and was well suited to entertain the children who invariably found a three-hour whale-watching trip sickening or tiresome or both.

"Ticket sales?" he asked.

"Perfect," she said.

They were not perfect. They were well below average that day, but she didn't want him to worry. The sales would be slow until the sun broke free of the cloud ceiling. It was not fog, though many called it that. It was the marine layer that had covered the Pacific coast more or less every day of every year for thousands of years, and burned off at about noon every day of every year for thousands of years. But the tourists could not grasp this or did not believe it.

The *Seeker* took two trips each day, one from nine to noon and one from two to five, and even though the morning trip was always in calmer seas, and was more likely to yield whale sightings, it was invariably underbooked. The tourists woke up, saw the gray skies, and figured the bay would be cold and rough. But it was not. Or it was, but only for the first hour.

CLEAR SKIES EVERY DAY AT 10 A.M.—GUARANTEED! Hazeemah had written on the chalkboard outside the ticket booth. "What do you think?" she asked.

Hazeemah had been handling the ticket booth for twenty-two years and had a face like a painting. Her eyelids were thick and heavy like those of a Renaissance muse. When she'd applied for a job with Marv back when, she'd hoped to be out there on the water as a naturalist or photographer, but had gotten violently ill every time she stepped onto a boat, tethered or at sea. Her parents were from Kashmir, and she insisted that people of that region were missing some key cochlear bone crucial to sea-steadiness.

Since then she'd helmed the ticket booth, and Aurora had grown up helping her, or pretending to help her. When Aurora was ten, Hazeemah showed her how to work the register. When she was sixteen, she counted on Aurora to set up the website and upload photos.

"Can we say 'Clear skies every day'?" Aurora wondered. "Seems like some kind of contract."

"You could write that," Marv said, "but you probably shouldn't." Hazeemah assessed her handiwork and Marv's recommendation. She had been chastely, vaguely in love with Marv for a decade but now was dating a chef based in Salinas. She erased the guarantee. Promise or no, the water was invariably less choppy in the morning, which meant that the tourists would be less likely to get sick. When they got sick, they went online and wrote bad reviews, blaming Aurora for the movement of the ocean.

CALMER SEAS IN THE MORNING! Hazeemah wrote on the chalkboard. GUARANTEED.

"That's probably fine," Marv said.

The three of them went into the ticket booth, a wood-framed shack on the Monterey dock. Hazeemah worked behind a narrow plywood counter, using a decade-old laptop and an even older inkjet printer. The walls around her were covered in photos of whales and orcas and dolphins. Aurora was in many of them—as a stringy-haired, sunburned girl at her father's side, as a teenager in mirrored sunglasses and braces, as a young woman settling into her bottom-heavy body. Sturdy, someone had once called her, not unkindly. She'd played lacrosse in high school, and her coach had urged her to throw her hips around. Which she had.

"The fish looks wrong," Hazeemah said. Above the counter was a fake swordfish, and once a month Hazeemah became unsatisfied with its position.

"It's a fish, not a painting," Marv said. "It'll look right however you hang it."

Hazeemah stepped back. "He looks depressed."

"Maybe move his head up like he's jumping?" Marv said. Hazeemah angled the fish's head upward.

"Now he's euphoric. Don't change it, Zeem," he said, touching her forearm gently. Hazeemah smiled with her bright, small teeth.

"How many do we have?" Aurora asked.

"Eleven so far," Hazeemah said. "Here comes your coffee. Hi Portia."

Portia was in the doorway, a striking silhouette in a tank top and long suede skirt. Tall and angular, she made her own jewelry from copper and fake feathers, and sold it on the boardwalk. She was among thirty or so tablers that set up their wares every morning. There were tie-dyed-T-shirt makers, spin-art demonstrators, leatherworkers, landscape painters, and a half dozen artisans who specialized in anamorphic creatures made from driftwood and rocks. Portia's jewelry was on the high end of the pier's price-and-quality spectrum.

"I'm late," she said, and handed Aurora her coffee. There was a good café on the ground floor of Portia's apartment building, so she'd been bringing Aurora her order for years. Portia was squinting at the fish on the wall. "Why's it crooked?" she asked.

"Don't," Aurora said.

Hazeemah shimmied out from behind the counter. "I knew it."

"Zeem, it's fine," Aurora said. "Portia, stop."

"He looks sick," Portia said. "Is he supposed to look sick?"

Hazeemah took the fish off the wall entirely.

Aurora followed Portia back to her table. "Idiot. She believed you. She's very sensitive."

"The fish was actually crooked," Portia said.

"Are these new?" Aurora asked, pointing to a row

of silver hoops with tiny feathers attached. "Are these pigeon? I'll only wear pigeon."

"They are new. And they're not pigeon. Quit touching."

A tall man wearing jeans and a sleeveless denim jacket—the sleeves seemed to have been violently detached—was setting up his table next to Portia's.

"New?" Aurora mouthed.

Portia mimed the quick zipping of a mouth.

The new man presented as a cowpoke or biker, and had jagged handwriting tattooed on the back of his bald head; it looked to Aurora like a doctor's prescription. She thought about opening with that, a question about skin art and pharmacology, but she assumed Portia would be displeased.

"Hello sir," Aurora said.

The man turned, revealing a face haggard in the cheeks, bright in the eyes. He was handsome in the way a gnarled tree might be, with two blue gemstones pressed into his ancient bark.

"Hello to you, too," he said. "Woodrow." He extended his hand, which was as heavy and variegated as a quarried stone.

Aurora hadn't thought of what to say next. She glanced at his table, where she gleaned that he made, or at least sold, belt buckles and knives. "I wonder if you can help me. I need a belt buckle and I also need a knife, but my budget is tight. So I was wondering if you have any buckles that are *also* knives?"

Portia dropped into her chair and hid her head in her hands. Woodrow looked down at Aurora through his tiny blue eyes.

"No, I'm fresh out of buckles that are also knives," he said. "Which makes me seem like a bad business-man. People will be asking the same question all day."

Portia had caught Aurora's eye and aimed a bony finger-gun at her.

"Anyway," Aurora said. "Have you met Portia?"

"I have," he said, "last week. Hello again, Portia." He mimed the tipping of an imaginary top hat. From most men this would have meant a hard stop, but he made it work.

"Don't you have a boat to steer?" Portia asked, and Aurora spun back to the dock.

From her bridge Aurora honked the horn, a booming but jaunty salute, just as her father used to. It was a way to bring attention to the boat and the business, to alert indecisive tourists to the idea of whale watching. This day, a few dozen heads turned toward the sound, squinting to find its source, but none of them seemed moved to buy tickets. Her father poked his upper half through the door, holding a plush dolphin.

"Got yourself a toy?" Aurora asked.

"I thought maybe we'd have a trivia contest. Just for the kids. The winner would get this," he said. These were the ideas he liked most—extra touches, promotions, games, or the occasional joke or anecdote he'd relate over the loudspeaker. Not that his extra touches had any effect on ticket sales. A text came through from Hazeemah. *Thirteen tickets sold*. The bare minimum to break even was fourteen.

In Aurora's two years in charge, there had been no significant setbacks, but she hadn't grown the business, either—an outcome that surprised her. She'd expected to have doubled the revenue by now. She'd done two years of business administration at Cal State and had modernized aspects of the operation, but the profits had flatlined. Either her father had been a far better businessman than she'd assumed, or she was a bit worse than she'd expected.

Deitz poked his head into the bridge. "Ready?" he asked, and Aurora nodded. Deitz was a lanky former firefighter of thirty-two, with intense, assessing eyes and a close-trimmed beard. He was Aurora's steady and calm right hand, overqualified for his role, handy with engines and navigation and people.

Deitz's girlfriend, Fiona, worked the merch table and snack bar down below, an oddly profitable part of the business. Passengers got onboard and immediately bought snacks for double what they would have paid on the pier; after the tour, if they'd seen a whale, they wanted a shirt to prove it.

Fiona, a petite Latina from Pacifica, had been with the *Seeker* for five years, though Aurora wasn't quite sure why. She had a degree in physics from UC Irvine and talked vaguely about getting her PhD. Two years ago she'd met Deitz at a Phish show, brought him onto the *Seeker*, and now they were the backbone of the operation. They showed up together, on time, each morning, and did not leave until the last task was done. On their days off they climbed mountains and camped in the desert.

Deitz saw the plush dolphin in Marv's hand. "Who's that for?" he asked. "Not you, I hope."

On paper Marv and Deitz shared every interest; they were both practical and capable men, but they did not like each other much. There was no ease, no banter. Aurora had finally realized that Deitz was largely humorless. He made sharp-edged statements that attempted mirth but that made no one laugh. When he heard a joke, he only nodded.

Aurora checked the time. It was 8:32.

"Let 'em on," she said.

Deitz disappeared to the lower deck to drop the gangway. It was important to get those inclined to seasickness acclimated as soon as possible.

Aurora looked down the pier at the listless tourists wandering around the boardwalk. "C'mon, c'mon," she whispered to herself. She thought about honking again, but just then a family of five, who had been striding quickly toward the parking lot, stopped, engaged in a quick discussion, and finally turned around and walked directly to the ticket booth. Minutes later they were aboard, and with eighteen passengers, Aurora pulled into the bay just as the first rays of sun broke through the cloud cover, an hour earlier than usual.

This day, as on most days, Aurora was the first out. Tulia, the *Seeker*'s naturalist, tapped her microphone and began her narration, a well-rehearsed mix of warnings, cetacean facts and musings on the goings-on beneath the surface of the sea. "Welcome aboard the *Seeker*, and get ready for a day of unimaginable beauty. Relatedly, if any of you are feeling sick at any time, do not go inside the boat. That is the very worst place to be. Stay outside and make your way to the stern, where you can empty your stomach into the sea and feed some grateful fish..."

Declan, captain of the *Lazy Day*, was usually second out, and he was in no rush; that was part of his brand. Declan's tours were looser and boozier; his T-shirts read YOU GOOD. WHALES GOOD. ALL GOOD. Aurora and the *Seeker* emphasized education and family fun, while Declan sold his passengers on a Jimmy Buffet spin. *Have a margarita, see a whale. Or not. Have another margarita*. The *Seeker* didn't have an alcohol license and Aurora didn't want one. Drunk people on a boat were a towering liability and gave a captain no peace. But it was a lovely arrangement, with Declan's and Aurora's clientele never coming close to overlapping.

"As we make our way out of Monterey Bay," Tulia continued, "you might see some moon jellyfish. Their sting is quite painful, and there are thousands of them, which should give you further disincentive to jump overboard..."

Tulia had no training as a naturalist, but she did have a degree in poetry, and once a month the crews of the *Seeker* and the *Lazy Day* were invited to hear her read. She was a small-framed woman of thirty-four, with thick hair the color of cherrywood and a pensive, lipless mouth. Over the years her poetry had evolved, from unmemorable free verse about trees and snow to, lately, very graphic, and loud, descriptions of sexual encounters she hoped to have in the near term.

Aurora picked up speed and saw the *Lazy Day* pulling out. For decades there had been a third whale-watching vessel, an old ferry called the *Discovery*, but Len, the captain and owner, had sold the business six months ago to a mysterious buyer, and the *Discovery* hadn't been seen since. Word was that it was being refurbished, but Aurora wouldn't have been surprised if it had disappeared entirely. Whale watching was a family business, not a growth business.

After twenty minutes, Aurora's radio pinged. It was Declan. "Anything?" he asked.

"Nothing yet," she said.

The long-standing custom was for all three boats to alert one another to any sightings, and the system worked for all involved. Len would find something and radio Declan and Aurora. Or Aurora would come upon a pod and radio Declan and Len. Invariably, all three boats would gather in a loose arrangement around whatever they'd found, and all passengers would go home happy. Now, though, with one fewer boat, things were harder. It didn't help that Len had been the best spotter of them all.

This day, an hour in, Aurora saw a spout and steered toward it. When they came close, they saw that it was a humpback, about twenty-eight feet long. She pointed it out to Tulia.

"Folks, we have a humpback whale on the port, or left, side of the boat," Tulia said over the intercom, and the eighteen passengers on the *Seeker* rushed over to the port side. "The humpbacks are often called 'the guardians of the sea,' for the way they take care of other sea creatures. They've been known to warn sea lions of ships and to protect seals from orca attacks. The humpbacks have SP cells in their brains, which we have as well, and these cells have been associated with things like higher cognitive thinking..."

Aurora's father was at the railing, pointing to the whale, the plush dolphin in his hand. He signaled up to Aurora and Tulia, and then Aurora saw it, too. There was a calf, about two months old and white as a cloud, swimming next to its mother.

"Folks, this is rare and wonderful—we have a baby swimming alongside its mama," Tulia said, and Aurora knew the trip was in the bank. A mother and her calf was a royal flush, would be the highlight of the day, and she felt a great calm come over her. There were days she searched for hours before sighting even a dolphin, so this mother and child, an hour in, was a lucky thing, a gorgeous thing. She radioed Declan, and in seconds her father arrived back in the bridge.

"You radio Declan?" he asked.

"Just did," she said.

"You want to get closer?" he asked.

"I do," she said.

"I'll take the wheel."

Aurora went to the lower deck, greeting the passengers as she passed between their hushed and reverent forms, and then looked closer at the mother and calf. There was a vast sea around these whales, so the fact that this mother was swimming close to the *Seeker*, with her baby, meant—to Aurora, at least—that she was proud of her baby and wanted to show her off.

"So sweet," one of the passengers said.

The sun painted the waves gold and Aurora shut her eyes. Since she was a kid, she'd done this, closing them to the dancing light. She let the light soak her eyelids in pinks and purples and blues. With her eyes closed she could hear the mother's exhausted breathing, the push of air through the wet blowhole. In a kind of trance, she heard the slap of the waves against the hull of the *Seeker*, and listened to the passengers' awed murmurings and the digital clicks of their picture-taking, the groan of the vessel as it rose and fell on the heavy sea.

"You'll see our steady captain, Aurora, with her ear to the sea, her eyes closed," Tulia announced. "Just a reminder that seeing is key, but you can listen, too."

Aurora opened her eyes to find that most of her passengers had closed their eyes, even a pair of young sisters, no more than six; their smiles were beatific. Declan's boat arrived, and was soon gliding past on the other side of the mother and child. Aurora waved to him and he waved back. He seemed unusually giddy, red-faced and exuberant, and she thought he might be tipsy, too. His passengers all had *Lazy Day*–issued sippy cups full of tequila and sugar, and she was never sure if, out of camaraderie or compulsion, he drank on the job, too. If he did, it wasn't enough to cause anyone to notice. He'd never struck the dock or another boat, had never done anything odd or dangerous, really, so she never asked.

No, she said to herself. *No, no, never*. He would never risk all this, this life. There had been moments in her life when she had wanted more, when she was bored and suffocated and wanted to leave Monterey and see Rwanda or the Solomon Islands, or to join the

FBI or the Secret Service. A few years ago she'd had a pair of passengers, a husband and wife, who were both federal agents, and they'd told her how to apply, that it wasn't too late, that she wasn't too old.

But she didn't want to go back to school, not at forty-one. And anyway, once a month there was a day like this, when she doubted any other life could improve upon this, in its freedom and light, the hunt of it, and the hint of danger, and the faces from all over the world, all on her boat, trusting her to show them prehistoric mothers swimming in golden water with their cloud-white babies.

At the end of the day, Aurora docked the *Seeker*, Deitz tied up, the afternoon's tourists disembarked and twenty minutes later she was sitting with Portia at Bea's with matching margaritas. Deitz and Fiona had gone home; they were heading to the mountains to watch a meteor shower expected that night. Marv was sitting with Hazeemah and Tulia at the next table, the three of them sharing a pitcher of grapefruit juice and vodka. A text arrived on Aurora's phone.

Happy Birthday!

It was Carlos, an ex. He sent birthday wishes months early, months late. He didn't know any birthdays beyond those of his immediate family, he'd admitted, so he sent birthday wishes to Aurora whenever something reminded him of her.

Saw a pumpkin and thought of you.

This was lewd, about her ass, about the hard roundness of her oversize ass; he'd been the only one to appreciate it this way. She smiled. She and Carlos had dated on and off since high school, and he'd been both loyal and noncommittal, both steady and exasperating in his lassitude. He showed up but made no plans on his own. He was both affable and passive, both capable and lazy.

Aurora tapped back. *You're thirteen weeks early.*

I wanted to be first, he wrote.

Because you're thoughtful.

I AM thoughtful. Where are you?

Boat.

Any blues recently?

Carlos had a thing for blue whales, though he'd never seen one in person. They were not so rare on this coast in the fall, but it had been a strange season thus far. Lots of humpbacks, no blues.

No blues. A humpback and calf today, she wrote.

"Is that Carlos?" Tulia asked. "Tell him I said thanks."

"For what?"

"He was the only one of you losers that bought my last chapbook."

"You have a new book?" Hazeemah asked. "Is it sexy? I'll buy it if it's sexy."

"Tell him," Tulia said again.

"You do it," Aurora said, handing her the phone.

Aurora thought of Carlos's loose, bowlegged walk, his narrow hips, his hard belly. He was an enthusiastic lover but initiated nothing. When they'd dated, he never said no. At the slightest indication from Aurora, he'd made himself instantly naked, said things like *Wow* and *Oh man* and *Yeah baby*, didn't care if he was on top or she was, didn't really care what happened. He was thrilled to be involved in any way, and always finished in minutes. And immediately after, he wanted to talk about something entirely unrelated, some news he'd been waiting all the while to tell, like a lightning storm he'd seen in the mountains or some weird feature of his body he'd just noticed.

"Is that Carlos?" Marv asked. "Say hi from me."

"She's got my phone," Aurora said, and nodded to Tulia.

"Tell him my collarbone's healed."

"I don't have the phone, Dad."

"And that I watched *Prison Break* like he said."

"Christ," Aurora said, and took the phone from Tulia and handed it to Marv. He and Carlos began a long thread involving inside jokes and photos of old ships and obese bears. Their relationship was far more joy-filled than the one she herself had with her father. Marv and Carlos delighted each other in a way that reminded Aurora of two toddlers in day care—a kind of first love.

"Where is he?" Aurora asked, but Marv was too involved to answer.

Carlos had been a teenage skateboard champion, a semiprofessional snowboarder, then spent the next decade catching his breath and engaging in a desultory journey through semi-employment. He'd worked in marine construction for a few years, and was part of the blowing up and disposal of the old Bay Bridge. After a year in the Monterey Planning

Office, Carlos had finally decided he wanted to be a long-haul truck driver. Now he popped into town every six months or so to see his family—a storied clan that had been in California since 1750 or so. They were among the first Californios, successors to the Spanish nobility who had been given land from Mexico to Oregon, and who sold it to the Americans coming west. Some returned to Spain, some stayed, and now Carlos's family owned a string of restaurants and a parking garage downtown.

"He's in Missoula still," Marv said when he handed her phone back. "He got a new rig. Twice the power as before. Twenty-four wheels."

"Don't they usually have twenty-four?"

"No. Eighteen. He's coming back in a few months. Did he tell you that?"

"That's what he told me," Hazeemah said.

"When did *you* talk to him?" Aurora asked.

"He's my friend, too," Hazeemah said, and stirred her drink with her finger.

"What the hell is that?" Marv stood up and moved toward the window.

"Kinda looks like the *Discovery*," Portia said.

A vessel the size and shape of the *Discovery* was coming into the marina, but this vessel was newly painted, an austere matte black with chrome trim.

"Looks like a concept sketch," Tulia said.

"Russian oligarch–style," Hazeemah said. "They like the matte black."

As the vessel drew closer to the dock, they could see that there was a man at the helm, wearing a black fleece vest, aviator sunglasses and what looked to be driving gloves. He docked expertly, maneuvering into the *Discovery*'s old slip as if he'd done it a thousand times. From within, two crew members in matching black fleece vests appeared and leaped like deer onto the dock. Their pants were cotton, salmon colored, their sneakers immaculate and white. They tied up and then disappeared back into the boat. Marv craned his neck to see the stern.

"They renamed it. The *Omni*," he said.

The name seemed an unnecessary lateral change from the *Discovery*, and was, more important, flouting maritime superstition.

"Bad luck to rename a boat," Tulia said. After years on the *Seeker*, Tulia had begun reading books about shipwrecks. There were far more than Aurora had thought possible.

Between the name change and the paint job, it was clear the *Omni*'s new owner was not a timid or subtle man. But was he at least cordial? After half an hour of preparations, the captain and his two-man crew disembarked and did not linger on the dock, and did not go to Bea's for drinks and tacos. They went directly to the parking lot, where they got into a large black SUV and drove off.

In the morning, Aurora arrived early to meet Deitz. He'd been hearing a strange knocking from the engine and wanted to take a look. By eight, Hazeemah was at her station and Aurora swung by Portia's table to get her coffee. Woodrow hadn't arrived yet.

"Twice divorced," Portia said. "He said each wife lasted fifteen years. Is that concerning? I don't like the symmetry. It feels too tidy."

"Like a pattern," Aurora said, and winced. She did not want to discourage any love Portia might find, so she tacked. "He's committed. He's steady."

Portia nodded, but Aurora pictured two great pyramids, a wife buried underneath each. She knew these pyramids were an apt and indelible image, one that she could not put into Portia's head under any circumstances.

"Whatever. I'm not marrying him," Portia said, as if Aurora had just insisted upon the idea.

A van arrived in the parking lot and Woodrow emerged. For a moment Aurora didn't recognize him. He had his sleeveless denim jacket on a hanger, and put it on as one would a dinner jacket.

"He hangs the jacket on a hanger," Aurora noted.

"Please don't say anything," Portia said.

"What would I say?"

"Actually, can you just leave?" Portia asked.

"I'll be quiet."

"No. I'm begging you to go."

When Aurora reached the *Seeker*'s bridge she saw that Declan was already on the *Lazy Day*. She waved at him, and he waved back and nodded toward the *Omni*, the site of a flurry of activity. There was a crew of five now, all with matching black fleece jackets and salmon pants.

Aurora radioed Declan. "It appears they have uniforms."

"It appears they do."

"They make any contact with you?"

"Nothing yet," Declan said.

She'd decided that she could forgive yesterday, but the right thing for this new captain to do, for him and his crew to do, would be to introduce themselves to Aurora and Declan on this first full morning of the boat's rechristening.

So for the next half hour, Aurora moved between the bridge and the dock, making herself visible and available. She made a point of loudly banging around the *Seeker*, calling out to Hazeemah in the ticket booth and greeting Tulia, who arrived at 8:20. But 8:20 came and went without any greeting, then 8:30 and 8:40, and with her own vessel filling and Declan's, too, it was suddenly too late for any pleasantries with the *Omni*.

She radioed Declan. "Still no word from the new people?"

"Nothing at all," he said.

And yet all morning, well-dressed young tourists had been boarding the *Omni*.

"How are they selling tickets?" Aurora asked.

"I hear online only," Declan said. "They have an app. And that code that looks like broken *Tetris*."

"QR code."

"Right."

Aurora shoved off at nine and went to her usual spots, expecting humpbacks, but found nothing, not even dolphins. She radioed Declan at ten.

"Anything?" she asked.

"For a while I followed what turned out to be a log," he said. "Have you ever followed a log for seven miles?"

"I have not."

"Wait. Look to your five o'clock."

Heading north, almost to Half Moon Bay, they saw the *Omni*—a tiny black rectangle on the horizon, like a censor's redaction. Aurora grabbed her binoculars and saw that the *Omni* was stationary, which meant they'd sighted something.

Marv poked his head into the bridge. He still had the stuffed dolphin.

"Damn it," she hissed.

"What?" he asked.

"The new boat found something."

"So?"

"They didn't radio."

"Don't be so proud. Just go there," her father said.

She couldn't and wouldn't. The *Omni* hadn't invited them, and her pride wouldn't let her simply sidle up to it uninvited. Instead, she went north and, at a quarter after ten, she found a group of white-sided dolphins who jumped at the bow for a few miles. That was all for the day. No whales. It was Tulia's job to sell whatever they saw.

"Folks, this is very rare," she announced, adopting a tone of hushed awe. "This time of year, to see such a friendly and playful pod of white-sided dolphins..."

It wasn't so bad that her passengers would ask for their money back, but still, if the *Omni* had been following custom, the day could have been good for every boat, every person.

"What do you think they saw?" Hazeemah asked.

They were all at Bea's, watching the *Omni*'s customers disembark. Aurora had already had a glass of sauv. blanc and planned an imminent switch to a margarita. Portia was abstaining, determined to go the week without. She'd been experimenting with various deprivations—gluten, carbs, legumes.

"What if Denim shows up?" Aurora asked.

"Woodrow."

"Do we like his name?"

"We do. If he shows, then I drink," Portia said.

The *Omni*'s passengers continued to disembark.

"So young," Tulia noted.

"Their sneakers! They're too clean," Hazeemah said. "I see so many clean sneakers and think of cults."

"We should flag the captain down," Declan said.

When the *Omni*'s passengers had left and the crew, now seven strong, had cleaned up, they made their way down the dock and, as before, went directly to the parking lot. Finally, the captain walked down the gangway, taking off his gloves, one finger-pull at a time.

"Should we call him?" Hazeemah asked. "I think we should." Hazeemah had the air of a shy person but was not shy. She would speak to anyone at any time. She ran to Bea's balcony and yelled down to the *Omni*'s captain, "Come on up, mystery man!"

The captain, startled for a moment, lifted his index finger and then went back to the *Omni*, as if he'd just forgotten some urgent item. He remained inside for fifteen minutes.

"He wore the gloves again," Declan said. "You ever wear gloves?"

"Never have," Aurora said. "Dad?"

Marv shook his head. "I had a bandage once," he said, and raised his left hand. "It kind of looked like a glove."

"And the pants," Tulia said. "Are those capris? They don't cover his ankles."

"Is he still in the boat?" Aurora asked.

"He just left. Wait. Here he comes," Hazeemah said. "Jesus Christ. Finally."

When the captain entered Bea's, he engaged in a purposeful conversation with Lily, the hostess, who led him back to Louis, the bartender. While he and Louis spoke, the captain's eyes scanned the restaurant's ceiling and floors with machinelike precision.

"He's sizing the place up like a building inspector," Declan said.

"You think he's a building inspector?" Tulia asked.

"He's not a building inspector," Marv said. "Building inspectors don't take thirty tourists out on the water just to surprise a restaurateur."

Tulia accepted this and rested her chin in her palm, watching the captain as he and Louis appeared to exchange phone numbers.

The captain was a thin, athletic man of about forty, with carefully cut salt-and-pepper hair, a square but delicate jaw, and liquid brown eyes that seemed free of all trouble. Aurora pictured him in a Sharper Image catalog, barbecuing asparagus on a solar-powered grill. Finished with Louis, he made for the door.

Hazeemah gasped, and rose halfway from her chair. "He's supposed to stop here. He's not stopping. He has to stop, right?"

Tulia's eyes, scandalized, turned to Aurora.

"Fine," Aurora said, and all but cut off the man's path to the door. "Don't run away just yet," she said, trying to seem amiable. Up close, his face was smoother, softer than she'd expected. Now she thought mid-thirties, late thirties. Thirty-seven. She was sure he was thirty-seven. "We're all in the same business," she added. "Come say hi."

He looked from Aurora to the table where the mixed crew members of the *Seeker* and the *Lazy Day* had gathered. As he took in their sunburned faces and Hawaiian shirts and colored drinks, his head dropped a quick but definitive inch. It was the slightest movement but it was not missed by anyone. It conveyed, abundantly, that the idea of stopping to talk with Aurora and her coterie was a catastrophic waste of his time. Still, he pivoted and walked toward them, extending his right hand.

"Brandin with an 'i'", he said, and he shook everyone's hands the same way—one tidy motion up, one tidy motion down, then release.

"Sit," Aurora said.

Brandin blinked twice and shaped his mouth into a stiff smile. "Unfortunately, I'm running late."

"One drink on us?" Declan asked.

"Another time," Brandin said, and waved both his hands at waist level while backing away.

"Hold on," Declan said. "What'd you guys see today?"

"Pardon?" Brandin said.

"What'd you see out there? Gotta assume you saw something. You were in the same spot for forty minutes." To underline the offhand nature of his inquiry, Declan took a long pull on his Modelo, though he kept his eyes on Brandin.

Brandin's mouth dropped open just a bit, but no words emerged. It was as if he couldn't decide if answering Declan's question would reveal some proprietary secret. Finally he reapplied his stiff smile. "We saw a pod of orcas feeding on a dead humpback. The whale was about thirty-one feet. We have pictures on our socials if you want to..." He took a few steps backward and again did the waist-level wave.

Now Declan stood and set his beer down loudly on the table. "Hang on," he said. "You're new, so it's something we should explain. Out there, the three boats share intel about where the whales are. It's been a courtesy extended for decades by everyone in the business, including your predecessor, Len. Len was our friend, and we actually pioneered this system with him, so..."

Declan did not think it necessary to finish the sentence, but Brandin was looking at him blankly, so Marv stepped closer to Brandin. Marv tended to touch the forearms of anyone he spoke to, and Aurora was afraid he would do so now, too.

"We just mean that if you see a whale, you let the other boats know," he said. "It's more fun for everyone that way. Easier, too."

Brandin looked at Marv as if he'd found a scuff on his car and didn't have the tools to remove it. Then he squinted briefly, signaling that Marv's information had been processed and filed.

"That's an interesting perspective," he said, and then stepped around Marv and made his way to the door, careful not to touch a thing.

"Motherfucker!" Aurora said. She was alone in the bridge. Weeks had passed, but the moment at Bea's still came to her with alarming frequency. *Interesting perspective.* How could those two words be imbued with such condescension? Her blood boiled when she heard either word in isolation, and she shuddered when she saw that matte black finish on anything else—TVs, Teslas, bike locks, water bottles.

Brandin and the *Omni* continued to go about their business with no contact and no courtesies. They arrived at 8 a.m., shoved off at 9 a.m., and returned at 12. Their passenger load was uniform; they never had more than thirty-two passengers, never fewer. And every day, during and after their trips, they posted an eerily steady array of sightings—orcas, grays, humpbacks. Their social feeds were cheerful, even exuberant. *Three humpbacks today! All breaching! Grateful! Come join us next time!*

Marv couldn't stand it. It broke him open. After that evening when Brandin stepped around him, Marv had tried a few more times to engage the *Omni* and its crew, to no avail. He even boarded the vessel one morning with a basket of fresh lemons he'd picked from his garden, and was politely ignored until he left. He got so upset that Aurora worried about his heart and sent him home. He hadn't come back since.

Declan radioed. "You see him out there?"

Aurora looked to find the black redaction of the *Omni* holding still, a few miles west.

"I do," she said.

"So you think we give up on them? I'm ready to give up."

"I already gave up," Aurora said.

Declan gave up, and Aurora got better at ignoring the *Omni*. Instead of trying to compete with its socials and matte black finish and what she presumed was some kind of satellite-aided whale-searching system, she doubled down on the family-business aspect of the *Seeker*, the faded wooden ticket shack, her witty poet-naturalist and local crew. The *Lazy Day* offered two-for-one drink tickets and free chips and guacamole. Business was not much worse than before, and things fell into a new kind of balance—a joyless kind of détente.

One morning in mid-October, five weeks after the *Omni*'s arrival, Aurora got to the boardwalk at eight and found it empty. There was no Portia. No Woodrow. There were no artisans at all. Instead, there were two young cops drinking coffee.

"Where are the crafts tables?" Aurora asked.

Their name tags said OCHOA and O'CONNELL. Ochoa was in the middle of a sip. He finished and waved his hand in front of his mouth.

"Too hot," he said.

"I told you," O'Connell said.

Aurora remembered them. They were the two officers who had found her father asleep in his car. They had been gentle with him—unusual for young cops, who otherwise seemed perpetually on edge.

"So where are they?" Aurora said.

"They were told to go," O'Connell said.

"By you?" Aurora asked.

"Yes, by us," he said. "Technically, they're not supposed to be here. None of them had permits. Which actually surprised me."

"Is it red?" Ochoa asked his partner, and extended his tongue.

"It's pink. It's supposed to be pink," O'Connell said to him, then turned to Aurora. "I didn't know this before, but apparently none of these merchants had the right paperwork, and even if they did, they're not supposed to be blocking egress here." He gestured around the boardwalk, which was wide and empty.

"But they've been here for a hundred years," Aurora said.

Now Declan was at her side. "What's happening?"

"They kicked out all the artists."

"You can't do that," Declan said. His tone had a sharpness to it that the cops did not appreciate. Ochoa looked over the top of his cup at Declan. "Excuse me?"

“Declan, these guys were just acting on orders,” Aurora said.

“Ma’am, that’s incorrect. We were *not* just acting on orders,” O’Connell said.

“I just meant that it wasn’t your decision.”

“We enforce the laws,” O’Connell said evenly. “You’ve heard of the words ‘law enforcement’ before? Those two words together?”

“I have,” she said.

“So we enforced the law today,” he said.

“But what happens to them?” Aurora asked.

“Who?”

“The craftspeople.”

“They apply for permits, I’m guessing.”

“But then there’s the egress issue,” Ochoa added.

“There is that,” O’Connell said.

Aurora looked around, as if for a third cop, a judge, someone with the power to turn back time. She saw Portia’s red Subaru at the far end of the parking lot. “See you later,” she said to Declan and walked over to Portia. Her upper half was bent inside the trunk, arranging crates and boxes and her folding table.

“Those fuckers,” Aurora said. “We’ll fix this.”

Portia crawled backward, stood up and turned to Aurora. Her face was splotchy, her eyes red. "The cops were fine, actually. They said they had complaints from other businesses on the wharf. As if we're vagrants. No one ever said anything about permits before. I've been coming here since 1998. Before those cops were born!"

"What can I do? Want to come out with us?" Aurora asked. "Come for a ride on the bay. Don't be alone. Or go with Declan. He has drinks. Or you can drink on my boat."

"Nah. I'm heading home. I have to go look at the city website for the laws and permits and all that shit, I guess." She got into the driver's seat.

Aurora held the door ajar. "It has to be the new guy."

Portia stared at her steering wheel, then looked through the windshield and found the sun. "Hell. It's a clear day, too. Business would have been good."

"I'll make some inquiries," Aurora said. She eyed the *Omni*. "I'll fix this."

Aurora strode over to the dock and saw a figure in the *Omni*'s bridge. She cupped her hands and yelled, "Hey!"

The figure did not turn. Two of the crew members were washing the spotless deck. Aurora ignored them and walked up the gangway. She climbed the teak stairs to the bridge, passing another deckhand, a young, fit woman with dark eyes, tasteful makeup and a ponytail. "Can I help you?" the woman asked.

"You cannot," Aurora said, and kept climbing.

On the top deck she saw Brandin standing behind the bridge's plexiglass. She tried the door and found it locked. She'd never encountered a locked bridge before. Only off the coast of Somalia did captains lock their doors.

She knocked on the window. Brandin did nothing. Aurora stopped breathing. Over the course of her life she had come to expect that when she knocked on a door, or a window, the person visibly inside would immediately come to the door, would smile, would greet her, would apologize for the delay. But Brandin did not look her way. This was behavior she'd never seen in person, hadn't thought possible.

She knocked again, now with the heel of her hand.

For the briefest moment he seemed to tilt his head just an inch, as if some force within him were suggesting turning toward her, a fellow human knocking loudly on his window. But he overrode this instinct and kept looking at his iPad.

Aurora, outraged, knocked louder. She knocked with her knuckles, then her open palm. Brandin pulled a stool up to his console and sat down, making himself more comfortable as he assiduously studied his iPad.

Aurora saw that beyond the *Omni*, Declan was watching her. His hands were raised and splayed, as if he were ready to leap the hundred feet from his bridge and onto the *Omni*'s deck to come to her aid.

"Hey!" she yelled again at the glass. Now Brandin was making a call. He seemed very serious, his eyebrows almost meeting above his nose, and then hung up and placed the phone facedown on his console.

Aurora, feeling volcanic, sat back on the railing, staring at Brandin.

And now he was looking up. At her? Not at her. At someone approaching her from behind. He lifted his chin as if to say hello.

"Ma'am."

She jumped, almost screamed. She turned to find the two cops she'd met earlier on the pier. They were flanking her, as if ready to take her away.

"Ma'am, you have to stop banging on the glass," Ochoa said.

"I wasn't banging on the glass," she said stupidly.

"The captain of this boat called to make a complaint. You should probably leave if you don't have a reason to be here," O'Connell said.

And then she was being led gently away, down the teak steps, past the deckhand with the ponytail, whose eyes registered that she'd never seen anything so barbaric in all her life. Aurora was guided off the boat, and once they were on the pier, O'Connell took out his notebook. "You say you own a business here, ma'am?"

"We met less than an hour ago."

"I know, but—"

"I'm the captain of the *Seeker*. I've been here longer than you've been alive," she said.

"Why does everyone keep saying that to us?" Ochoa asked. "You're like the fifth person today. I'm thirty-three, so..."

Aurora had to regain some leverage. A lie arrived. "I was missing a cooler today," she said, "and I looked on the deck of the *Omni* and saw an identical cooler on their deck. So I walked over to ask if his crew had mistakenly borrowed it. Actually, I should be making a complaint myself."

O'Connell wrote this down carefully, lifting a forefinger periodically for her to allow him to catch up. Ochoa was looking very seriously at her. He believed her, and this gave her immeasurable strength.

"And was your cooler actually the one you saw on his boat?" he asked.

"I still don't know," she said. "He wouldn't open the door."

"He didn't answer the door?" Ochoa asked. This seemed to be a red line crossed. Aurora relished this, loved this young man. She assumed he was local.

"Did you try calling him?" O'Connell asked.

"I don't have his number," Aurora said. "And I didn't think I needed to. I was standing right in front of him. Among us captains, there's usually a certain courtesy—"

"Would you like to file a report of, like, burglary?" O'Connell asked.

The balance of power had been reversed, and this new idea, of filing a report, was intoxicating to her. "Maybe," she said. "Maybe later. Probably. I'll see how it shakes out. Again, there's usually a certain courtesy extended between—"

"One would think," Ochoa said. "It irritates me when people call the cops instead of opening the door to talk. Like you said, you're a fellow captain, so..."

Aurora loved this cop named Ochoa with all her soul. O'Connell put his notebook away.

"In the meantime," he said, "can you stay away from that guy's boat? The..."

"The *Omni*."

Ochoa made a sour face. "Right. *Omni*."

"I will," Aurora said. "Gladly, I will."

Aurora had two days of low-level bliss, so happy about this temporary victory that she felt like all balance would be quickly restored in the world.

But then Brandin stole Fiona and Deitz. After a day when the *Seeker* and the *Lazy Day* witnessed four humpbacks and two orcas, the weather clear and warm, Deitz tied up and Fiona packed up the snack bar. Aurora went to Bea's with Tulia and Declan and Hazeemah, and in the middle of their first round, Deitz appeared. He handed Aurora an envelope and walked quickly to the parking lot, where Fiona was waiting by their camper-van. Inside the envelope was a formal letter of resignation. It began, "Dear Ms. Mahoney," and in it, he and Fiona informed Aurora that they'd been hired by the *Omni*, at a "significant pay raise," were excited to "begin their life's next chapter," and though they were willing to give Aurora the customary two weeks, they would prefer to move over immediately. Aurora looked up. Deitz was still in sight, strapping a mountain bike to the roof of the van. She called him on his phone. She watched him look at the call and decline it.

No need to come back, she texted. *I don't know what good riddance means, but it seems apt now.*

The next day, Deitz and Fiona were on the *Omni*, wearing the uniform vests and their personally improvised versions of the salmon pants; they hadn't had time to buy the correct brand. And true to the way of the *Omni*, all morning, they never looked at Aurora, said nothing to Aurora or Tulia or Hazeemah, their friends for years. They never waved. Aurora radioed Declan. "You see them?"

"I do. In the fleece. You know, I always thought those two were a little bougie."

"But why not be friendly? Why not wave?"

"They think you underpaid them."

"When?"

"For years. The whole time. I guarantee it."

"But they made more than I did!"

"You know these kids. They don't know how revenue works. They think there's some well of money unrelated to tickets and merch. And now they get paid better by Brandin so they think you cheated them."

"Oh Christ," Aurora said.

"They're not doing real math over there. They have a crew of eleven now. It's absurd."

"Who do you think's funding that operation?"

"No idea. But let it go." The radio clicked off.

Aurora looked out at the ocean. It was devoid of all interest that morning, a slate sea with a white roof.

Declan radioed again. "Sorry, I know that's stupid. That fucker stole two of your best people. You should be angry. But don't be angry."

"Okay," she said. She very much wanted to quit. Or to call the police. What could Ochoa do about this? She wanted to at least ask. She wanted to hear that this kind of thing irritated him.

"How are your ticket sales today?" Declan asked. "I'm at six. A bit dispiriting."

Aurora called Hazeemah.

"Ten so far," she said. "It's dead out here."

Aurora looked down the boardwalk. The day was windy, colder than usual.

Hazeemah called back. "I can do the snack bar," she said. When Aurora protested, Hazeemah said, "I'll be fine. I'll close up and take four Dramamine. Oh wait. I have one more customer. Hello, sir. Just one, sir?" Her tone had turned familiar, joking. "See you in a sec, Aurora." She hung up.

Tulia popped her head into the bridge. "Remind me: When do I let people on?"

The crew was scrambling to fill the gaps left by Deitz and Fiona.

"How about now?" Aurora said.

"Now. Good. Okay. I will." She jogged down the steps to the pier.

Aurora took one more look at the boardwalk. She watched Hazeemah lock up the ticket booth and felt a simmering rage within her. All this was the doing of one person. He'd made a harmonious community into something fractured and ugly. He'd turned her friends against her and now he was forcing Hazeemah to get on a boat, where she'd almost certainly puke for the next three hours. Aurora was about to call Hazeemah and insist she turn back, but then a figure walked down the dock. It was Carlos.

Aurora laughed a barking kind of laugh. She couldn't believe it. He'd bought a ticket. She pressed her face to the glass, hoping he'd see her and come straight up. But he was hugging Tulia, and as he did, his old Specials T-shirt, brown at the armpits, rode up and exposed his hard belly. He'd never had a coherent personal style, and he'd gained some weight and lost some hair, but he looked as formidable as ever, fore-arms roped with veins, and finally he looked up to find Aurora in the bridge.

Aurora almost collapsed with gratitude. When an enemy comes into your life, all you need is an ally. Someone to balance the math. It was so simple. Carlos, thank god for you, she thought. Now there was this sweet, strong man who had always loved her, had never done anything but fall a bit short, and he was coming aboard.

"Hey pal," he said as he entered the bridge. She enveloped him, taking in his sunscreen and his Secret deodorant and his ham-smelling coffee breath. She locked her hands around his waist and squeezed his soft back so hard she expected to hear a click or a pop. He grunted and she released his waist but let her head rest against his. She looked down at his hard, round belly and sighed.

"Your dad made it sound like you needed a friend," he said.

"You have no idea," she said. "He called you?"

"Let me help out today, yes?"

Hazeemah stayed ashore and Carlos joined the crew. He helped run the snack bar and locate two humpbacks from a quarter mile away, a massive pod of leaping dolphins, and an orca's rainbow spout. Aurora watched Carlos move around the boat with an easy charm and she felt a swirling love for him that she needed to set free. When they came into the dock, Carlos jumped from the boat, tied it up quickly and masterfully, and after that the steps were almost perfunctory. She invited him for the usual drinks with her crew and Declan's, and after one drink she said she needed to get to bed early. He said he'd walk her to her place, and within seconds of opening her door they were entwined on the couch, and he pulled her leg over him and rested his hands on her waist.

"I like looking up at you like this," he said and lifted her shirt, burying his face between her breasts. They moved to the bedroom, where he was naked in seconds. He sat against the headboard and pulled her down onto him.

"I like this position. I could do this all day," he said, and in minutes he pulled out and climaxed on his stomach. Afterward he asked her to stay on top of him, straddled and naked. She leaned down to kiss the crown of his head, knowing he wanted to talk. He always wanted to talk immediately after.

"You seem okay to me," he said. "Your dad had me worried."

She put on her panties and sat cross-legged next to him.

"Where have you been, by the way?" she asked.

He described the last few drives he'd made—one to Toronto with a load of apricots, one to Maryland with a few thousand hubcaps—and all the while, Aurora thought about having him move in. It took everything in her to resist the urge to ask. But still. The idea seemed like a very good one: it was liberation; it was fleeing this horrific new world where a man in a void-colored boat circled her, taking her customers and crew and ignoring her as she hammered her hands against his window.

She could quit the whale-watching business and travel the world with Carlos. Not truck-driving traveling. Wild, flinging travel, reckless and well funded. He would do it, would do anything, had never said no to anything she'd proposed. She'd sell her business, he'd sell his truck. Who would buy the *Seeker*? The whole business? She mused about what price it might bring. The boat was worth two hundred thousand.

Maybe less. The slip, the license to do business on the wharf—that was another fifty or hundred thousand. The ticket booth was worth something. Twenty? So maybe three hundred total? She and Carlos could travel for three or four years on that—five if they were clever and frugal. And Carlos had money saved, too, no doubt. He was a good traveler, never sad, never moody.

"Look at this thing my tummy does," he said, and Aurora watched him create a deep diagonal crease in his stomach. "And my toenails are getting really thick, like my dad's," he said, and then another subject seized his mind. "Does this look cancerous?" He lifted his arm and pointed to a mole in the thicket of his pit-hair. He wanted her to examine every part of him. "Did I tell you I might be going to nursing school?" he finally asked.

"No, you didn't," she said.

"At Cal State," he said. "This time, in two years, I could be a nurse."

And Aurora came crashing back down again. She couldn't ask him to leave and travel the world. Carlos would be a nurse and that was good and right. And she would remain a captain of a Monterey whale-watching boat.

"Listen, I can't make it tomorrow," he said.

She remembered this, too. He rarely did anything two days in a row. He jumped into any work task, gave it everything he had, then took a day off.

"Is that a problem?" he asked, but her mind was floating away.

In the morning she was running late, and when she got to the ticket booth, Hazeemah was already there, but was standing outside, looking at her phone.

"See if it makes sense to you," Hazeemah said, and nodded to the door, which bore a red notice.

CONDEMNED UNTIL FURTHER NOTICE, it said. Aurora read the fine print. The document was from the city's building inspector, who had deemed the structure unsound and unsafe.

"Did you see who put this up?" Aurora said.

"It was there when I got here," Hazeemah said.

Aurora checked the time. It was 8:20.

"All my stuff is inside," Hazeemah said.

The notice prohibited entry into the booth.

"We're allowed to get our things," Aurora said, then she saw the padlock.

"That's why I'm outside," Hazeemah said. "Otherwise, I would have just gone in."

"Motherfuck," Aurora said. "We can't even go out today. We have no way to process the customers. The credit card machine's in there. Everything's in there."

And then she saw him. He was approaching from the parking lot. And Deitz was with him. Now they were commuting to work together?

"Aurora, don't," Hazeemah said.

But Aurora was already striding toward the two men in their fleece vests and pink pants. It seemed Deitz had gotten the right brand of pants. They stopped short of his ankles, and somehow this sent her over the edge. "Was this you?" she roared.

Brandin kept walking, saying nothing. Aurora walked alongside Deitz.

"Do you know your boss somehow managed to get my ticket booth condemned? Does that seem good to you? Does that seem ethical and neighborly to you?"

Deitz gave Aurora a quick death stare, then picked up his pace.

"What happened to you, Deitz?" she asked. "You think your new boss would get Phish's approval? You think Jerry Garcia would like Brandin? Do you? You've become one of their little faceless robots, huh? A *henchman*! You're a henchman!"

"And you're a hysterical lady."

"Hysterical lady? I'm a hysterical lady?" she yelled.

"One that underpays her staff," he said, and pointed at her with both index fingers.

"Really? You think you got me there? Do some math, moron. You think I'm a fucking millionaire? Looking at ocean mammals? I'm secretly hoarding all the snack bar money?"

Now Hazeemah was in front of her, pulling her away. "You know what kind of sexist punk calls a woman hysterical? You can't even do math, you fucking henchman! You fucking wormy little henchman!"

Hazeemah was trying desperately to stop Aurora from following them.

"And what happened to Fiona, by the way?" Aurora yelled to their backs. "I see she's not with you. Was she hysterical, too? Now you have your fleece bro and don't need a hysterical lady around? Is that it?"

Deitz turned around and walked backward, smiling. "She's parking the van, Aurora," he said. "And I think you need help."

Hazeemah was now sitting on the dock holding Aurora's arm like a child trying to save a kite from flying away in a storm. She looked up to Aurora with pleading eyes. "Stop. For me?"

"What do you do, Brandin?" Aurora yelled. "You go around filing little complaints to the city? Like some little bureaucrat?" The two men were now at the *Omni*. "There goes the bureaucrat and his henchman! In their matching pants! How many pairs of pink pants do you have now, *henchman*? How many?" she yelled as they stepped aboard. "No one wants you here, do you know that? This is a place for actual humans! Not fleece robots in matching pants! You hear me? Do you?"

The morning was a mess. The passengers' names were inside the ticket booth, and the waivers, and the credit card processing machine. Aurora took a full boat out, having no proof anyone had paid. By noon Hazeemah had made an arrangement with Bea's to use their credit card processor, and had decorated a borrowed sandwich board with the basic details of the *Seeker*'s operation. Six people signed up, and though the trip was a loss, Aurora refused to concede the day.

She needed Carlos. She called but he didn't pick up. He didn't answer texts. Without him she was short-staffed, and worse, she did not have a steady, large-bodied man next to her who would say, "Fuck those fucking fuckers." She needed that most of all.

But he didn't answer all morning, and she began to hope he'd been in an accident—something minor but involving the fire department. Any other excuse was inadequate. *Urgent*, she texted. *Just write back*.

Declan found a pod of orcas and radioed Aurora. She motored to him as if he were Moses. "Thank you, thank you," she said, as her passengers took pictures.

All day she called Carlos but got his voicemail and had the crushing sense of having depended on a man who did not want to be depended on. They were both over forty and she hadn't learned—he'd been undependable at seventeen. At twenty-two. At thirty-one. Now at forty-two. That's why he'd taken up truck driving. He had no boss, no coworkers. He had to deliver containers to their destinations on a schedule, but otherwise he was alone and free.

After work she went to Declan's house. His sister Glynnis was in town; she'd done two years of law school somewhere in Oregon.

"She knows a lot," Declan said.

Glynnis had dimples and wild graying hair and wore a hemp poncho. She made iced tea and gin for the three of them. "In terms of Deitz, I don't suppose you have a noncompete in your employment contract?" she asked. "Maybe he's giving away trade secrets?"

Aurora laughed. Declan paced the kitchen, wondering aloud which of his own staff might be poached.

"Go outside if you're going to do that," Glynnis said. "Use the trampoline."

Declan went onto the deck and began jumping on a fraying exercise trampoline. He left the sliding glass door open. "We can take turns if you want," he said.

"No thank you," Aurora said, and watched him jump. He had an unsettling lack of rhythm.

"This ticket booth thing is a major step," he said, breathing hard. "This is an..." He gasped, stopped. "This is an escalation."

"You could sue him," Glynnis said.

"Sue him for what?" Aurora asked.

"Doesn't matter. Anything. Both of you sue him for different things. File a different suit every week. Make it hell for him. My ex has a private practice in Salinas and he'd do it. He likes to sue pricks."

Aurora smiled. She'd needed someone to articulate her anger and give her an action plan. She would not sue, had never sued anyone, but thinking of it cooled her molten rage into some sharp metallic shape.

"What's the name of the company again?" Glynnis asked.

"I don't know," Aurora said. "I assumed it was just the *Omni*."

Glynnis was online and in minutes had found something. "It says it's owned by an LLC out of Delaware."

"Delaware!" Declan said from the trampoline. "That's something."

"That's nothing," Glynnis said. "That's where basically all businesses are registered." She kept reading. "Man, the ownership is really opaque for such a small business. I think it's maybe a tax write-off? Whale watching isn't a cash business, is it?"

"Not so much," Aurora said.

"I bet this is one of those private-beach people," Glynnis said. "You know how a couple times a year some rich guy moves to California, buys a house on the beach and then tries to make the sand private?"

"They can't dooo that!" Declan sang from the deck.

"We know, you goon," Glynnis said, and turned back to Aurora. "This is the same kind of thing. These people don't like the way it is out here. The coast is open and messy and public—three things they can't abide. And didn't you say that Bea's had been visited by a food inspector?"

"Yesterday," Declan said.

"I didn't hear that," Aurora said.

"So we can kill them?" Declan asked. "I think we go straight to killing."

Glynnis ignored him. "I'll look up the local laws. He certainly did. That's how he got rid of all the craftspeople. But maybe he's violated some ordinance himself? It gives me something to do while you guys are out on the water."

Declan came in from the deck, his shirt dark with sweat. "You gotta leave now," he said to Aurora.

"I have to stop thinking about this bullshit long enough to sleep."

On the way home Aurora got a text from Carlos.

Sorry. I was with my family. Want me to come over?

No please no, she wrote.

When she got home, he was in the driveway. He'd ridden a bike and was fanning his armpits with his T-shirt. She let him in. He took a beer from the fridge, sat on the couch and pulled her feet into his lap.

"I'm sorry," he said. "I'm not a quick texter."

"But this is different, don't you think?" she said. "I mean, we're in the middle of a crisis. I just—" She looked at the ceiling and drained her eyes. "I mean, didn't you come back to help with this? My dad called you, you came back to help? Did I get that right?"

"I came to help, yes."

"But then you disappeared."

"Turn around."

"No."

"Please."

Aurora didn't want to do anything he asked.

"Hold on," he said, and crawled along the back of

the couch until he was behind her. He took her shoulders in his hands and began kneading.

"We needed your help today," she said. "You heard about the ticket booth?"

"I did, and I haven't been doing nothing. I talked to my friends in Planning, and this guy's part of a group trying to remake the waterfront. They say modernize, clean up, make it safe, family-friendly. But they mean make it less funky. Free it of all character."

"They have drawings and plans?"

"Models, schematics, all kinds of shit. They're organized. They've read all the zoning and bylaws. That's how they got rid of Hazeemah's booth. I mean, technically most of the buildings on the wharf aren't to code. He's probably coming for every old business on the pier."

"Jesus fuck, Carlos. Do we get a lawyer?"

"I don't know. But Ror..." He stopped kneading. His hands went soft on her shoulders, as if she were blindfolded and he were leading her out of a dark room and into some bright, celebratory place.

"What?" she said.

"Have you considered the possibility that you can't beat this guy?"

"Of course I have. Every minute I've considered that."

"You know your cousin, the Nowism guy?" he asked.

"Oh god. Not that." Aurora had a cousin who had accidentally invented a mini-movement. Nowism urged people to never, for a moment, look back. Every mind and muscle, every minute, should be engaged in uninterrupted sensualism, conflict-free. Something like that. Aurora didn't know much more about it, but she wasn't surprised Carlos did. He had a cousin who was a Scientologist.

"I'm just saying: Why fight this other boat? Even Marv is wondering if it's worth it. You sell the business, you'd do well. You could even sell it to the *Omni*."

"Oh Christ. You and my dad talked about that?"

"We did. We talk a lot."

"He'd sell the business?"

"He wants you happy."

"Carlos, this is such— I mean, what if someone tried to run one of your family's restaurants out of town? Like by calling the health department on them? All it takes is the whiff of suspicion and people will flee, right?"

"Right. That's my point," he said. Now he was lying back on the couch, holding a pillow to his chest. "This is a highly motivated and organized force here, and you have to think about how you want to spend the next few years. You could fight this guy every day, or you could leave the field of battle and do something else. A thousand other things."

"This is so strange coming from you. I mean, I know you're passive, but—"

"I'm *passive*?" Realizing that lying on his back seemed to prove the point, he sat up.

"Well, you're not, like, a man of action," she said.

Now he clambered off the couch. "Not a man of action. Okay." He went to the kitchen and put his palms on the countertop. "This is one of those moments when someone sums you up. We actually don't get these moments very often in life. This one I'll remember. Not a man of action. Right."

"Carlos. I didn't mean to summarize you. It wasn't a summary."

"It *was* a summary. That's what it was. You described it exactly right."

"This situation has me saying all kinds of weird shit. Deitz called me hysterical today, did I tell you that? I called him a henchman." Aurora came up behind Carlos and wrapped her arms around his stomach, pressing herself to him. "One of the things everyone loves about you is that you're kind. You've never hurt anyone, never hurt me. I'm the asshole—holding it against you that you won't go to war with this stupid *Omni* fucker."

He pushed her arms down and twisted his hips, as if getting out of a harness.

"I'll see you tomorrow," he said.

"You don't have to come," she said.

"I'll come," he said. "I told Marv I'd come."

In the morning Carlos was there before Aurora, and when she saw him, he nodded to the Coast Guard boat tied up behind the *Seeker*. On the dock, a lean captain with a concave chest and wraparound sunglasses approached. She knew him but couldn't place how. His name tag said MARINAO.

"Aurora Mahoney?" he asked.

"Yes," she said, and his first name came to her. "Russ. You know me. We were on the same float on the Fourth. The Captains of Monterey. Remember?"

His posture softened a notch.

"Right. Right-right. Well, good to see you again. I'm sorry about this, Ms. Mahoney, but—"

"Aurora. You've called me Aurora before."

"Okay. Aurora. We have reason to believe that your engine is not up to code, and might present a risk to your passengers. So we have to do a spot inspection."

"The engine's fine," she said. "It was just fixed, actually." And then it hit her. Deitz. He'd done this.

"You know we can board any vessel at any time," he said. "And we're responsible for the safety of—"

"I do know that," she said. "So you're coming aboard now, or what?"

"We're waiting on our engine specialist."

"Okay. So can I go out for my morning trip? It's nine to noon. Can we do this at lunch?"

"Aurora, you know the answer's no. You can't go out until we give you a clean bill of health."

Declan arrived, looking hungover and carrying a baby-blue cooler. "What's happening?"

"Are you Declan Rundgren?" Marinao asked.

"You know him, too," Aurora said. "He was on the float with us."

Marinao was no longer interested in personal overlappings. "Mr. Rundgren, are you the captain of the *Lazy Day*?"

"You know I am, Russ," Declan said. "Aurora, what is happening?"

"Mr. Rundgren, are you under the influence of alcohol at this time?"

"You know I'm not," Declan said, and Aurora's soul shattered, thinking that he very well might be. Good god, what if he wasn't sober?

"Test me," Declan said, and Aurora was saved from the abyss.

Marinao spent a long moment looking at Declan. "We can't do that without probable cause, and I have no probable cause."

"Good," Declan said.

"But we can't let either of you out on the water with passengers today. We've got a list of concerns and complaints about each of your vessels, from your engine, Aurora, to questions about dead-end wires and serving underage passengers for you, Declan. I need to interview your crew."

"We can't lose the day," Aurora said. "You know what that means to us?"

"I do. I know you'll miss a day's revenue. I do know that. But think of the greater loss if something were to happen to your engine while you're ten miles out. Once our specialist gets here, we can take a look and make sure you're tip-top."

"And when does this specialist get here?" Aurora asked.

Marinao checked his watch. "They said he was coming down from Alameda, so two hours, max. But you, Declan, we can start with your vessel now."

Over Marinao's shoulder, Aurora saw a minibus arrive in the parking lot. It was silver, with tinted windows, and from it she saw a salmon-colored leg emerge. They'd gotten their own bus.

Aurora had violence on her mind.

Then, from behind the bus, she saw a man approach on a bicycle. It was Carlos. He swerved skillfully, and the crowd of *Omni*s parted to let him by. He was wearing the same stained Specials T-shirt. He rode past the *Omni* crew, swung his leg over the bike frame and strode down the boardwalk until he reached Aurora and Declan and Marinao. He flung the bike over his shoulder, his sunglasses nestled in his shimmering hair. "Russ?" he said.

"Carlos?" Marinao said.

"I haven't seen you since Steve's thing."

They embraced and exchanged a series of claps on shoulders and chests.

"We went to Hong Kong together! Merchant Marine," Carlos explained. "How's Gus?"

Marinao shook his head. "Gus is dead, bro."

What followed was for Aurora and Declan a confusing and unsettling half hour, during which Carlos and Russ caught up, while the crew of the *Omni* went aboard and began preparations to go out as the only whale-watching vessel that day. Once Carlos became aware of Marinao's plans for the *Seeker* and the *Lazy Day*, he tried to bend Russ toward some semblance of mercy, but Marinao was hamstrung. He had orders, and his own crew had orders, and he couldn't abandon two missions at once just because he'd run into an old friend. This was at least the gist of it, as far as Aurora could glean. But it was clear, too, that Russ Marinao's posture changed entirely once he knew Carlos was part of the *Seeker* and friendly with the *Lazy Day*. The inspections would be pro forma, and the remedies rational and forgiving.

Aurora went to Bea's for breakfast and Carlos met her there. He took her hands in his. "I told Russ this was a setup," he said. "He believes me."

"But Jesus Christ. This is real now," Aurora said. "The other stuff was passive, bureaucratic. But this is something else."

"I know."

"I'm so sad."

"I know."

The *Omni* went out, and Aurora and Declan spent the morning watching the Coast Guard's young crew sift through the *Lazy Day*, finding very little of interest apart from a bilge that needed emptying and a bathroom that smelled of vomit. Marinao seemed apologetic, but they still had to wait for the engine specialist to come down from San Francisco, and when he arrived,

Marinao took him aside for a minute or two before he went down into the *Seeker*'s engine room, and he emerged twenty minutes later, with a shrug.

Aurora signed some forms and that was that. By the time the inspections were done, the sun had set, and between the *Seeker* and the *Lazy Day*, they'd lost about three thousand dollars in revenue. The Coast Guard left, and Aurora and Declan and Carlos were sitting at Bea's, drinking stiffer-than-usual margaritas, when Declan's phone dinged.

"Shit," Declan said.

"What?" Aurora said.

"Shit-shit-shit," he said.

"What? Speak!" Aurora said.

"They saw a blue," he said.

"Who?" she asked, but then she knew.

"Those motherfuckers," Declan said. "They're posting it on their socials."

For a while, everyone at Bea's watched the gorgeous footage of the blue whale, easily seventy feet long, swimming magisterially along the Monterey coast. *Stunning blue whale today! Grateful!* the post said. *Join us next time! #Blessed*

While they watched the videos on various phones, Carlos said nothing—only breathed slowly through his nostrils like a bull. He turned to look out at the water and saw the *Omni* on the horizon. It would dock in fifteen minutes.

"I can't be here when they come in," Aurora said.

Carlos stood slowly and squinted out at the sea. He still hadn't spoken.

"I'm heading home," he said finally.

"That's all you have to say?" Aurora said. "You're the one who always wanted to see a blue whale, and those fuckers impound our boats and then go and find a blue themselves. And you say nothing?"

She wanted anger from him. She needed rage. She needed a fighter by her side. But his face was serene.

"I'm sorry, you two," Carlos finally said, placing a heavy hand on Declan's shoulder. "This is very unfair to you both. It's a terrible thing that's happened here. But remember what I said: You have just the one life, and there are a thousand other things to do, a million other things to see. You don't have to stay here and fight this."

He leaned down and kissed Aurora on the crown of her head. He paid their bill and left.

In the morning, Carlos was gone.

He sent a text. *I'm sorry Aurora. Had to get back to Missoula. Will give a shout once I get there.*

He wrote again at midnight.

Arrived. Exhausted. Sorry to leave like that. Will write you more tomorrow.

But he didn't write the next day, and Aurora did not care. She was finished with him. She loved him and always would, but at that moment, the only humans she wanted in her life were warriors. She wanted to fight. She wanted to murder. She wanted lawyers, injunctions, cease and desists, civil suits, criminal investigations. Hazeemah showed herself to be fierce and angry every day, and Aurora loved her for it. Tulia was steady and simmering, and insulted the *Omni* and its minions every day, in wry bons mots delivered from the side of her straight, lipless mouth.

The week after the blue whale was uneventful, just a notch above miserable. There were no more inspections, no more surprises. They started their tours again, for Aurora refused to leave the field of battle. Meanwhile, she called lawyers. Glynnis made calls. They printed flyers and postcards and left them all over town. Business rebounded.

Aurora and Hazeemah had worked out an arrangement where customers bought their tickets inside Bea's, and ticket sales were respectable. They decided they did not need the ticket booth, not for the time being at least. All they needed to do was to stay alive while they worked out what to do about the *Omni* and their own lives. Especially in light of Declan quitting.

He'd come back to work on Monday and Tuesday after the blue whale, but the *Lazy Day*'s business was down—some new online reviews hinted at scandal—and on Wednesday at 4 a.m. he sent a text to Aurora.

I'm out. Take my passengers today if you can. I have four. Four! I can't fight anymore.

Then, a few minutes later:

All the joy is gone. So I'm gone.

For the rest of the week, Aurora took on the smattering of passengers who had paid for passage with the *Lazy Day*, and otherwise the vessel remained docked. The sight was hopeless, so sad Aurora couldn't look in that direction. Next to it was the *Omni*, and every day it was full, every day thriving with its matte black finish and its cold and violent separateness. Its passengers were cut from the same cloth as Brandin and his staff. None of them ate on the boardwalk. None of them had a drink on the wharf afterward or coffee before. They didn't set foot in any of the local businesses, treating the boardwalk as an unpleasant but unavoidable passageway between their Ubers and the *Omni*.

And finally Aurora weakened and broke. She began planning her own exit. She had not expected to live a life of conflict. Who pilots a whale-watching boat to exist in tense opposition to a force of bureaucratic aggression? She was disgusted with it all. The ugliness of it. The wharf was ruined, the sea was wretched and the sky had been made filthy and oppressive. She wanted to be gone. She stopped taking new reservations. She had to honor twenty or so sprinkled over the next few weeks, and after that, she was done.

When Aurora pulled into the dock one Tuesday afternoon, she found her father waiting for her. He was smiling. Hazeemah threw him the line and he tied the *Seeker* up. "Carlos got in touch," he said. "Don't roll your eyes. He feels terrible."

"I care not," Aurora said.

"Well, he's extended a grand gesture," Marv said. Carlos had arranged for the crews of the *Seeker* and the *Lazy Day* to have a box at the Giants game the next night. Everyone was welcome, everything was comped.

"Not interested," Aurora said, though she was actually very interested. She needed badly to leave Monterey for a day, a week. She'd never been in one of those boxes at the stadium where the food was good and free and you had your own servers and couches and a bar where you could pour your own drinks.

"He's got a block of rooms in a hotel nearby. Also free. Something his uncle booked for some clients. Apparently a whole contingent from Tokyo canceled last minute. I want to go."

"Then go."

"I think you need it, Aurora. I need it. I've never been to something like that."

"You go, then. Go. Go see the baseball game."

Marv worked on Hazeemah and Tulia. He called Declan, and Declan called Aurora.

"I'm in," Declan said. "I haven't left my apartment in a week. You should come. Please come. I'm fucking so depressed I'll kill someone. Glynnis is making me go. But I want to go, so she's not actually making me."

"This is fucking stupid," Aurora said.

But she agreed to go, even though it was such a moronic thing to do, to go on an all-staff excursion at a time like this. But the moment they were on the road, everyone piled into Tulia's minivan, Aurora felt a soaring liberation. The waterfront had become a squalid place for her, with the source of all her rage floating in front of her in physical form, a massive black blight on her conscience, a void into which all screams disappeared.

Leaving the wharf felt like a cleansing. With every mile they traveled north, she felt stronger, her mind clearer. When they crested 101 and saw San Francisco spread out before them, the lights coming on in the ballpark below, she thought she might just move up there. See whales from the Golden Gate. How hard could that be?

Marv got a text. "Carlos wants us to take a bunch of pictures and send them to him. Aurora, smile." He took a picture of her scowling, and he continued to take pictures all night—as they entered the stadium at Fourth and King, as they stepped into the box, as they gorged on garlic fries and pizza and drank and drank.

Aurora quickly got tipsy and watched very little of the game. She didn't recognize any of the players—she knew the name Buster, though there was no Buster playing that night—but was momentarily transfixed by a pitcher who appeared sometime in the middle innings. He was a tall, gangly man from Alabama, with a backwoods haircut and missing teeth on either side of his mouth. The crowd cheered for him in an outsize way, given that he seemed to be a recent arrival, and a middle reliever at that.

And soon the game was over and they'd taken two dozen pictures and hugged one another, and she and Declan had cried a bit, thinking of the life they'd had before the *Omni*, how lives can be perfect and then abysmal and hate-filled, and there can be very little done about it. Should anyone spend years fighting a terrible, immovable force when you could simply leave? Leaving felt so good. She felt giddy with the ways she might start anew. The FBI! It was time to look into that.

A pair of pedicabs pedaled them to their hotel, and they chatted for a long time with the front desk clerks before going to bed in their rooms overlooking the Embarcadero and Yerba Buena Island. The electronic door clicked loudly behind Aurora as she fell into the crisp white sheets. While using the headboard to steady her drunken spinning, Aurora knew there was happiness elsewhere, so much happiness all over. And this wonderful bed! Maybe she could live in a hotel like this. She'd travel the country with the FBI, staying in gorgeous and clean new hotels like this. It was not cowardly to leave. It was rational. It was a forward step. It was logical to begin again. Blind drunk, she texted Carlos. *Thnk U. Wonderful night. You were ri.*

Carlos's phone received this message in Missoula, but he didn't see it when it came through. Carlos was on the California coast, 1,200 miles from his phone. Earlier that day, he'd left his phone at his Missoula cabin, and had gotten into a semi driven by his cousin

Gordon, heading to California with a load of aluminum siding. Carlos rode in the bunk above the truck's cab, and was seen by no one. He was a ghost.

When they got to Half Moon Bay, Gordon dropped Carlos off on a dark stretch of highway, and Carlos walked to the waterfront, where their cousin Julian had left an old Boston Whaler, unregistered and unknown, in an obscure inlet, with two lumpy garbage bags inside. In one bag was a hooded wet suit and goggles, and Carlos put on the wet suit and steered the Whaler an hour south to Monterey Bay. It was just after 2 a.m. To anyone on shore, he would be a silhouette piloting a nameless and numberless boat in the darkest hours of the night.

But he saw no one.

Approaching the Monterey dock, he cut his engine and coasted toward the *Omni*. He tied the Whaler to the stern, slipped into the water in his wet suit, and swam under the *Omni* until he reached the dockside. He briefly emerged to untie the bow and stern lines keeping the *Omni* tethered to the dock, then swam back to the Whaler. He climbed back in and started the engine. After a few minutes of tugging, he was able to pull the *Omni* away from the dock and into the open bay. He knew security cameras would catch a shadowy figure, in a wet suit and goggles, emerging briefly from the bay to free the *Omni*, but identifying him would be impossible.

The water was exceptionally calm that night, and with a low cloud ceiling hiding the moon and stars, the dark was a velvet absolute. Carlos towed the *Omni* directly west, hoping he would not encounter the odd tug or yacht or patrol. But he saw no one, and while the Whaler's engine strained and grumbled, he dragged the *Omni* five miles into the Pacific. Land was only a black ribbon decorated with a few dim lights.

He steered the Whaler close to the *Omni*, tied up, and boarded the vessel carrying the second bag his cousin had left him. This one contained seven sticks of M1 dynamite, a twenty-foot fuse, and an activator. The M1 was five years old, left over from the job he'd helped out on, blowing up the old Bay Bridge. He dearly hoped the dynamite would still work. But with that much explosive, he did not need it all to work, and did not have to be clever about its placement; he only needed to make the largest possible hole in the hull of the *Omni* to send it quickly to the ocean floor. A boat like this would be prohibitively expensive to raise, impossible to repair.

Inside, the *Omni* looked like the private screening room of a nouveau riche millionaire. There were blond-wood floors and matte black surfaces. There were television screens on virtually every wall. He found the steps down to the engine room and the hatch to the bilge. He crawled to the rear corner of the bilge, near the engine, figuring a hole there would help the vessel sink quicker. He set the sticks in a tidy row, like seven sleeping soldiers, and unspooled the fuse. He'd decided on a long one, as he needed to give himself enough time to leave the *Omni*, get back on the Whaler, and speed out of range.

Once out of the bilge, he crouched briefly in the engine room, wondering if he'd forgotten anything. He'd been thinking about doing this since the first night he'd seen Aurora and Marv distraught by this cursed vessel. He knew he had the dynamite, had been keeping it for an occasion to be determined, and when he saw the rancor and misery Brandin and the *Omni* had conjured, the solution seemed only logical. But for a while he had hesitated, knowing the radicality of the plan, the insanity of it.

But then the blue whale had come. That crime had taken him to another place, sent him to a plane of white-hot certainty that the *Omni* was a tumor that had to be excised. A blue whale is a miracle, and a miracle can't be hoarded. A miracle must be shared.

So he lit the fuse. The hiss of a real fuse is far less dramatic, and far quieter, than the kind seen in films. And it's faster, too. Carlos's heart spun as he knew it was too late to reconsider; the fuse sparked and raced toward the bilge as he hustled back to the Whaler, untied it from the *Omni* and motored away. His chest was rattling, his stomach hollow.

He'd hoped to watch the explosion, but the fuse burned so quickly that he was still darting away, his back to the *Omni*, when he heard the blast. The sound was a hollow thump, and he turned to see the briefest white flicker, like a camera's flash, in the *Omni*'s lower level. In the next few minutes, there were a few hisses and shushings as air pockets collapsed, but otherwise the *Omni* disappeared without drama, silently, in a minute or two.

When it was gone, he motored over to where it had been moments before, but saw nothing. No spirals on the surface of the water, no sign of a vessel ever having been there. The continental shelf fell off steeply on this part of the coast, and the *Omni* was on a mile-deep journey to the ocean floor. He felt a surge of bliss and let out a breathy whistle. He had not expected this kind of elation; it felt like he'd beaten cancer. He looked up to the low gray sky and wanted to stay there, above the sunken ship, all night. He'd never be able to tell Aurora about this, as much as he'd have liked to. For so many years after this night, he would ache to tell her. To prove to her that he could make a grand plan and see it through, out of love for her and Marv and all that was impractical and untidy about the California coast.

But it was better to keep her free of any association with this night, and drifting over the falling ship, he knew it was time to go. He had to get south about seven miles and meet up with Gordon again. He motored quietly through the dark, and a thousand yards from land, he removed a battery-powered drill from the Whaler's glove compartment and put a one-inch hole in the hull. Sinking the boat would eliminate one key clue. As the water bubbled through the hole he'd made, he tossed the drill into the sea. The water rose around his legs and when he was knee deep he jumped off the Whaler and swam to shore.

He met Gordon on a lonely stretch of Highway 1 and they drove back to Montana. Gordon had delivered his load of aluminum siding, and was carrying a load of redwood timber back to Missoula. As before, Carlos kept himself hidden in the bunk above the cab, unseen by any other motorists or cameras, and he woke up as Gordon pulled into his driveway. He returned to his cabin and his phone, and enjoyed the photos that Aurora and Marv and everyone else had sent from the game. The Giants had won.

Brandin arrived at the dock in the morning, and for a long time he stared at the spot where the *Omni* had been. He called Deitz and asked if he knew anything. But Deitz was still in his van, in the parking lot, listening to Joe Rogan. After getting Brandin's call, Deitz rushed to join him on the pier, and the two of them walked up and down the wharf, expecting to see the *Omni* somewhere in the harbor.

Once in a great while, a vessel this large gets unmoored, by accident or on purpose, and barring a tsunami, one hundred out of one hundred times, such a vessel travels no more than a quarter mile. But never does such a vessel disappear.

The *Omni*, though, had disappeared. Brandin and his crew called the Coast Guard; Russ Marinao answered and knew nothing. They called the sheriff, the police, all the local fishing companies, and asked if anyone had seen an errant whale-watching vessel anywhere on the coast. No one had. It made the evening news and the next day's paper.

When police checked the pier's surveillance footage, some details emerged. At 3:21 a.m., a figure could be seen untying the *Omni* from the dock. But the camera, attached to the dock and with a limited perspective, couldn't see Carlos approaching or leaving in his Whaler. A casual observer might infer that, after the shadowy figure freed the lines, the *Omni* had simply drifted off, sailing over the edge of the earth.

The police investigated, the sheriff looked into it, but anyone with a motive had an alibi. Aurora, Marv, Hazeemah, Tulia, Declan and his crew—everyone had been at the Giants game, and there was endless photographic evidence to prove it. Most important, none of them had any idea who had done this. Carlos had told no one beyond his complicit cousins. The police reached Carlos by phone, but he was in Montana, and his phone's location indicated that when the *Omni* vanished from Monterey, he'd been asleep in Missoula.

Brandin, though, knew that someone had done this. Someone had stolen his ship. Over the next many months, Brandin pressed the police to investigate further, and they had, but they found nothing. Brandin hired his own investigators, and eventually they did locate the *Omni*—seven miles offshore and a mile down, resting on the bottom of Monterey Canyon. The shifting sediment would eventually spit it out to the floor of the Pacific, where it would fall deeper and deeper, far beyond any hope of resurrection.

Aurora and Declan found that working together, without the floating redaction of the *Omni*, was grand

and lofty again, that there could be no better life than this. They decided to stay. Their crews agreed, and business returned to something like how it was before. The ticket booth was reopened, the crafts-people returned—they simply came back, the cops did not care—and Aurora hired a different young couple, this pair from Jackson, Mississippi, to work the snack bar and the engine. Marv returned, too, though only once or twice a week, because he was dating a younger woman and needed to save his strength.

At the end of a blustery day in March, with sightings of grays and orcas and leatherback turtles, Aurora and her crew, and Declan and his, and Portia and Marv and even Woodrow, were all at Bea's enjoying drinks when they saw a familiar figure approaching. He was wearing a collared shirt with no buttons and sneakers with no logo, and as he wove through the dinner crowd, he was careful not to touch anyone or anything. It was Brandin, and for the first time, he looked old and he looked angry.

Aurora was surprised, and almost impressed, by this directness from him. Until then his weapons had been bylaws and permits, zoning and avoidance. She was very interested in what he planned to say, and as he stood in front of their two tables, hands on his hips, all twelve members of the two crews turned their attention to him. Declan yawned.

"One of you sank my ship," he said.

"Fuck you," Declan said, and yawned again.

"I think *you* sank it," Hazeemah said. "Probably for the insurance."

"The vessel was uninsured and you know it," Brandin said, and Declan let out a loud squawk of a laugh that caused half the restaurant to turn. Aurora's heart almost burst. How could he have been going out with passengers without insurance? Maybe he had liability, but no insurance for the vessel itself?

"Holy shit," Declan said. "Really, really, holy shit. That is the funniest thing I have ever heard, and the greatest news the world has ever known."

"One of you did it," Brandin said.

His eyes, Aurora noticed now, were perfectly round, like a doll's.

"Coulda been orcas," Tulia said. "They've been sinking boats in the Atlantic."

"I heard about that," Hazeemah said. "They might have come here to do some, like, copycat crimes."

Brandin stood as still as a human can stand without imploding. "It wasn't an orca and it wasn't an accident." His voice was rising, and as it did it grew more fragile. Aurora worried he might really crack up. He seemed to be a broken man.

"You'll be discovered," he said, and nodded at each one of them. "You'll be found out. You'll be caught."

Declan let out a breathy whistle. "Well, Brandin, that's an interesting perspective. Aurora, do you think that's an interesting perspective?"

"I do," she said. "It really is an interesting perspective. See you around, Brandin."

The disappearance of the *Omni* was not investigated further. No one in the Monterey Police Department took particular interest, and no witnesses or informants came forward. But one cold dawn, six months after it sank, Ochoa woke up with a thought: Carlos. It had to be.

Ochoa's apartment had a distant view of the pier, and that morning he looked out at the purple bay and couldn't believe how obvious it all was. Only Carlos had the expertise necessary to have untied, towed, and blown up a vessel the size of the *Omni*. And Carlos had both the motive and the opportunity, and even if no one on the *Seeker* or the *Lazy Day* knew anything about it—and Ochoa had a hunch that none of them did—Carlos would have had plenty of people willing to help him carry out such a plan. He had thirty cousins in town, minimum, and friends everywhere. Would it really be so difficult for a trucker to get from Missoula to Monterey unseen? To go anywhere unseen? No, not so difficult.

Looking out as the bay brightened from plum to calico, the sun only a vague promise, Ochoa made a plan to call Carlos later that day. Just to sound him out. Sometimes a simple call yielded unexpected clues, soft spots in someone's story. He went back to bed, tingling and thinking, vaguely, that he should write something down. In the happy numbness of dawn, he'd been forgetting his early-morning inspirations, and planned to buy a notebook.

When Ochoa woke up again, the sun had come out, bright and swaggering and clear, and the pier was full of visitors. The two whale-watching boats were filling up for their morning trips, and Hazeemah's ticket booth had a line out the door. In the months since the *Omni* had disappeared, the dock was singing again, alive again, carefree and ragged again, and word was that blue whales had been seen in unprecedented numbers. They were showing their tails, showing their babies as they traveled exuberantly south through the cold, bladed sea.

Ochoa showered and ate and dressed, trundled down the bleached wooden steps that led from his apartment to the boardwalk, and all the while he had the nagging feeling of a dream misplaced. He'd woken up and had a thought, that much he knew. Some phone call he had planned to make? But now he couldn't remember, and he had the sense that it did not matter, that for a moment all was right. He showed his face to the sun, took in its heat and promise, and walked forward in urgent forgetting.

DAVE EGGERS is the author of *The Eyes & the Impossible*, *The Monk of Mokha*, *What Is the What*, *A Hologram for the King*, and *The Circle*, among other books. He is based in the San Francisco Bay Area.

NOTES & ACKNOWLEDGMENTS

The Ocean Is Everyone's but It Is Not Yours is the sixth story in *The Forgetters* series of mini-books. If all goes according to plan, these stand-alone stories will someday be part of a larger work. Exactly when this will happen, no one can be sure. Thank you to cover artist Annie Dills, and to copy editor Caitlin Van Dusen. Research by Christina Ferguson was crucial. Thank you also to Amanda Uhle, Amy Sumerton, and VV. And thank you to the gracious and lucky whale-watching captains and crews of Monterey and the Golden Gate.

BOOKS IN THE FORGETTERS SERIES

The Museum of Rain

Oisín Mahoney is an American Army vet in his seventies who is asked to lead a group of young grand-nieces and grand-nephews on a walk through the hills of California's Central Coast. Their destination is a place called the Museum of Rain, which may or may not still exist. A testament to family, memory, and what we leave behind. *Also check out the audio version, narrated by Jeff Daniels.*

The Honor of Your Presence

Winner of a 2024 O. Henry Award

A homebody niece and her adventurous, almost-British uncle begin to attend parties to which they are not invited—an innocuous lark that becomes a very funny and lyrical referendum on why humans congregate and celebrate. Named a Distinguished Story in *The Best American Short Stories*.

The Comebacker

In this comic, lyrical story, Lionel is a beat reporter covering the San Francisco Giants. When a new pitcher is brought up from the minor leagues, he shows Lionel a rare, even unprecedented, ability to see the beauty in the game he's paid to play.

The Keeper of the Ornaments

Cole lives alone, has no pets, and has grown accustomed to a home life of profound quiet (not to say tedium). When a raucous household moves into the apartment next door, Cole assumes he'll have to move. But his new neighbors, and their very odd cats, see him differently than he sees himself. A powerful meditation on forgiveness, grace, and the happiness of being called upon.

Where the Candles Are Kept

Two seemingly sullen California teenagers are sent to visit their uncle Oisín in rural Idaho one summer, and ponder their escape soon after they land. In this wry and suspenseful story, all three are forced to decide who and what they care about, and if they have any role in the saving of a life.

Sanrevelle

Winner of a 2025 O. Henry Award

A man named Hop, not too young and not too old, lives in a sinking skyscraper and works for a personal-injury lawyer who's slowly losing his mind. Every day Hop stares out at the tiny boats on the San Francisco Bay, wanting to be out there and not filing paperwork for a cloistered madman. Finally Hop goes to a rickety dock by the sea, seeking sailing lessons. He meets the singular Sanrevelle, a barefoot captain, who leads him out of a grievance-based existence and into a life of speed and cold and light.

Author proceeds from this book go to McSweeney's Literary Arts Fund, helping to ensure the survival of nonprofit independent publishing.

www.mcsweeneys.net

McSweeney's, founded in 1998, amplifies original voices and pursues the most ambitious literary projects.

WE PUBLISH:

McSweeney's Quarterly Concern, a journal of new writing

The Believer magazine, featuring essays, interviews, and columns

Illustoria, an art and storytelling magazine for young readers

McSweeneys.net, a daily humor website

An intrepid list of fiction, nonfiction, poetry, art and uncategorizable books, including the Of the Diaspora series—important works of twentieth-century literature by Black American writers